Miami HEAT

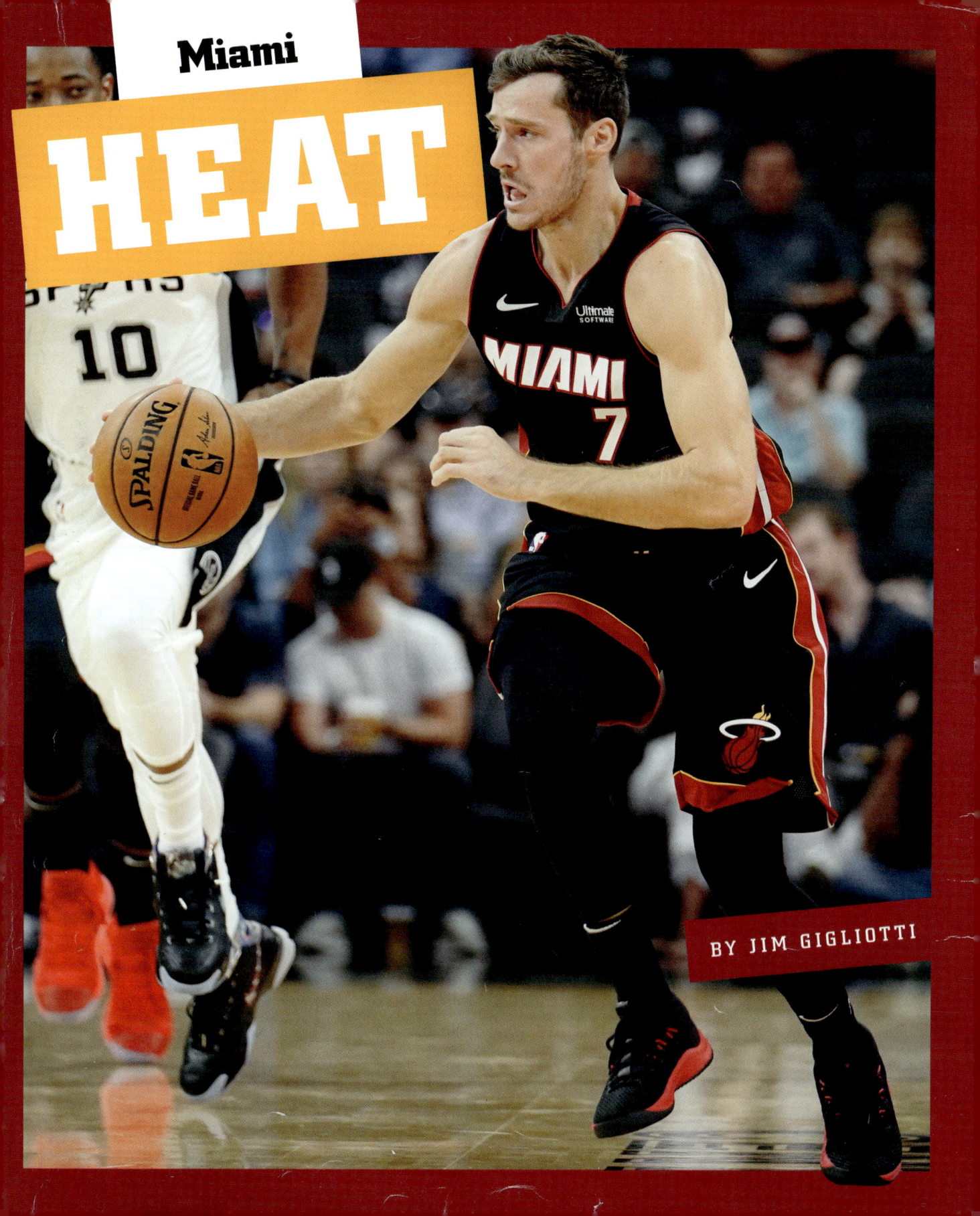

BY JIM GIGLIOTTI

The Child's World®
childsworld.com

Published by The Child's World®
1980 Lookout Drive • Mankato, MN 56003-1705
800-599-READ • www.childsworld.com

Cover: © Darren Abate/AP Images.
Interior Photographs ©: AP Images: Al Messerschmidt 9; David J. Phillip 17; Todd Essick 18; Wilfredo Lee 22; Joel Auerbach 26. Dreamstime.com: Massimo Campanini 13. Imgn/USA Today Sports: Steve Mitchell 5, 26; Jason Vinlove 26 (2). Newscom: Patrick Ferrell/TNS 6, 10, 25; George Bridges/KRT 21; Al Diaz/MCT 29.

Copyright © 2020 by The Child's World®
All rights reserved. No part of this book may be reproduced or utilized in any form or by any means without written permission from the publisher.

ISBN 9781503824577
LCCN 2018964287

Printed in the United States of America
PA02416

ABOUT THE AUTHOR

Jim Gigliotti has worked for the University of Southern California, the Los Angeles Dodgers, and the National Football League. He is now an author who has written more than 100 books, mostly for young readers, on a variety of topics.

TABLE OF CONTENTS

Go, Heat! 4
Who Are the Heat? 7
Where They Came From 8
Who They Play 11
Where They Play 12
The Basketball Court 15
Good Times 16
Tough Times 19
All the Right Moves 20
Heroes Then 23
Heroes Now 24
What They Wear 27

Team Stats 28
Glossary 30
Find Out More 31
Index 32

GO, HEAT!

The Miami Heat have not been around as long as many other NBA teams. The **franchise** played only its 31st year in the 2019 season. In that time, the Heat already have had a lot of success. They were a **dynasty** in the late 2000s and early 2010s. They won the NBA title three times. They are a top contender year in and year out.

Miami's Hassan Whiteside is perfect in pink as he slams home a basket.

5

Goran Dragic rises to the hoop in a key Eastern Conference game against the Philadelphia 76ers.

WHO ARE THE HEAT?

The Heat play in the NBA Southeast Division. That division is part of the Eastern Conference. The other teams in the Southeast Division are the Atlanta Hawks, the Charlotte Hornets, the Orlando Magic, and the Washington Wizards. The Heat have finished in first place 13 times. They have been to the **playoffs** 20 times.

WHERE THEY CAME FROM

In the late 1980s, the NBA wanted to add more teams. It wanted one of the new teams to be in Florida. The Sunshine State did not have an NBA team yet. The league could not decide between two Florida cities: Miami and Orlando. So it decided that each city would get an **expansion team**. Miami began play in the 1989 season.

In 1992, the Heat's fourth NBA season, Kevin Edwards tried to get past a Houston Rockets player.

9

Rodney McGruder leads the way as the Heat take on the Magic, a Southeast Division rival.

10

WHO THEY PLAY

The Heat play 82 games each season. They play 41 at home and 41 on the road. They play four games against each of the other Southeast Division teams. They play 36 games against other Eastern Conference teams. The Heat also play each of the teams in the Western Conference twice. When Miami plays Orlando, it is called the Sunshine State **rivalry**.

WHERE THEY PLAY

Miami has lots of nice beaches. Some fans thought the city's new team should be called the Sharks or the Waves. However, Miami also is one of the warmest cities in the United States. The Heat was a natural fit. Besides, a basketball player who is shooting well is said to be "on fire"! The Heat plays its home games at the American Airlines Arena in Miami.

An American Airlines airplane is painted on the roof of the Heat's home arena.

Palm trees line the entry to the American Airlines Arena, home of the Heat.

13

14

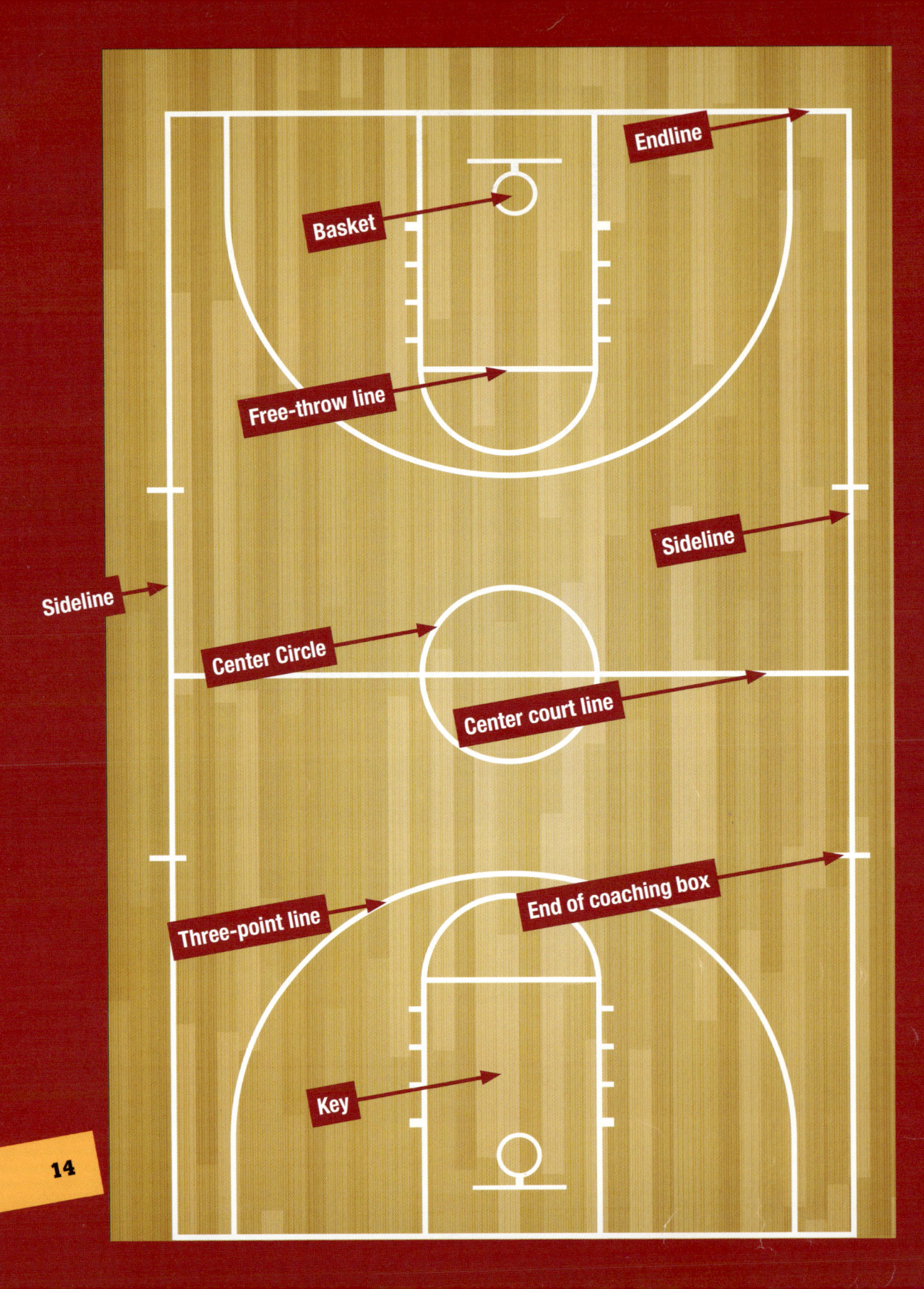

THE BASKETBALL COURT

An NBA court is 94 feet long and 50 feet wide (28.6 m by 15.24 m). Nearly all the courts are made from hard maple wood. Rubber mats under the wood help make the floor springy. Each team paints the court with its **logo** and colors. Lines on the court show the players where to take shots. The diagram on the left shows the important parts of the NBA court.

GOOD TIMES

The Heat lost the first two games of the 2006 **NBA Finals** to the Dallas Mavericks. No problem. Miami won the next four games for its first title. The Heat won 27 games in a row in 2013. Only two NBA teams have had longer streaks. The Heat won a team-record 66 games that season. LeBron James scored 61 points to help beat Charlotte in 2014.

17

Dwyane Wade holds the Most Valuable Player trophy he won for his play in the 2006 NBA Finals.

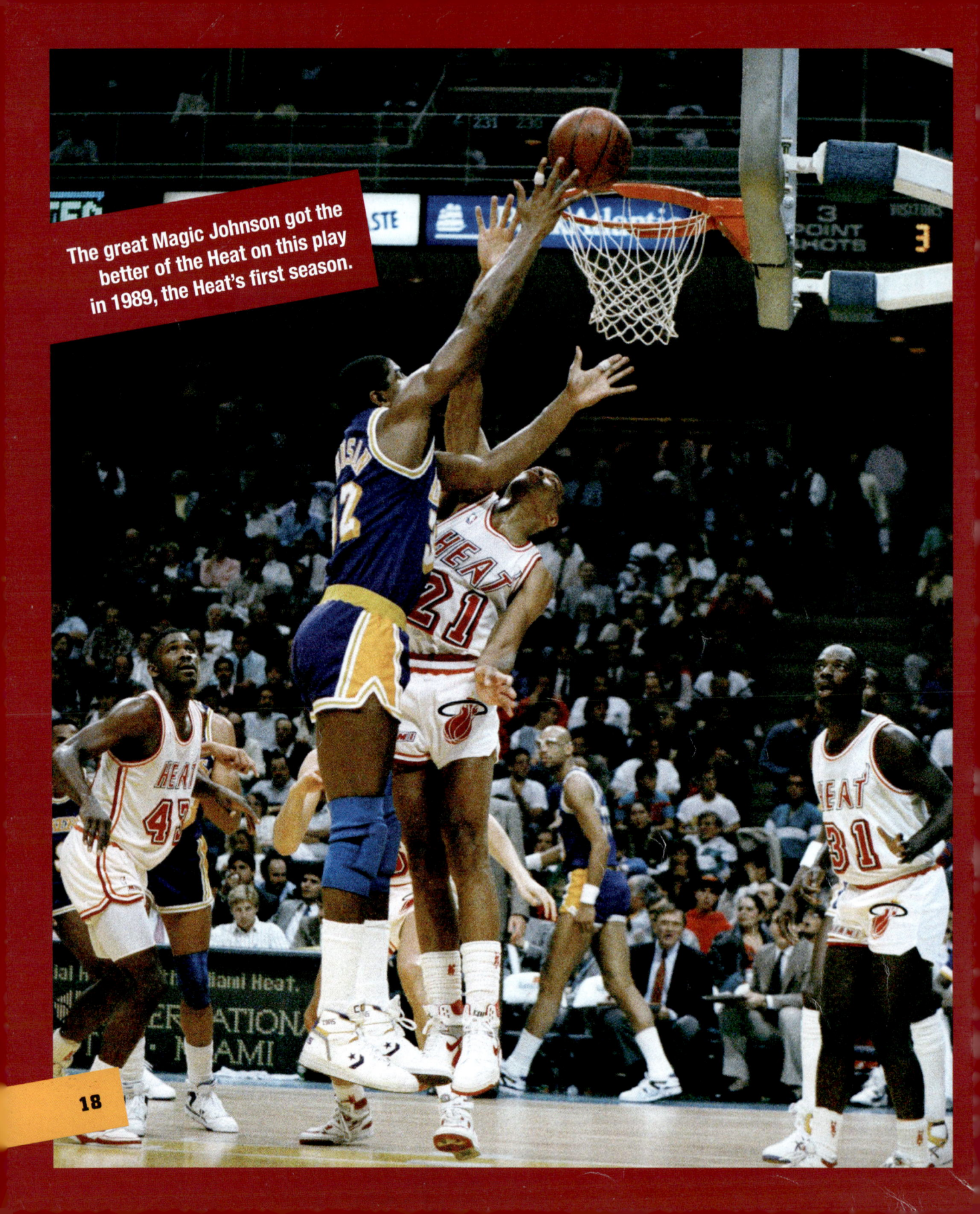

The great Magic Johnson got the better of the Heat on this play in 1989, the Heat's first season.

18

TOUGH TIMES

Most expansion teams have trouble at first. The Heat had even more than most. The team lost its first 17 games. It finished with only 15 wins. The team won only 15 games again in 2008. The Heat signed superstar LeBron James in 2011. They became a title contender again. In the NBA Finals, the Heat lost to the Dallas Mavericks.

ALL THE RIGHT MOVES

The drop step is a key move for a big man. He has his back to the basket. He takes a step back and to the side of a defender. Then he spins to the basket. Bam Adebayo's drop step for the Heat is a good one. No one had a better drop step than **Hall of Fame** center Shaquille O'Neal. It almost always ended with a soft layup or a slam dunk.

A "big man" in the NBA is not only a large, tall player. He is also a key part of a team's offense.

Heat fans were thrilled to watch one of the NBA's best dunkers, Shaquille O'Neal.

The "Big Three" of Dwyane Wade, LeBron James, and Chris Bosh helped Miami win two NBA titles.

HEROES THEN

The Heat drafted Dwyane Wade in the first round in the 2004 season. They traded for Shaquille O'Neal the next year. By 2006, the Heat were champs. LeBron James signed with the team in the 2011 season. Star big man Chris Bosh joined the Heat, too. They teamed up with Wade to form the "Big Three." They helped the Heat win two titles.

HEROES NOW

Dwyane Wade was the face of the Heat for many years. He played his last season with the team in 2019. Now it is time for others to shine. Josh Richardson took over Wade's old spot. He is the team's shooting guard. Center Bam Adebayo has long arms and quick feet. He is a tough defender inside. Justise Winslow is another great defender.

Josh Richardson is the Heat's scoring and playmaking leader.

25

Heat Uniforms

WHAT THEY WEAR

NBA players wear a **tank top** jersey. Players wear team shorts. Each player can choose his own sneakers. Some players also wear knee pads or wrist guards.

Each NBA team has more than one jersey style. The pictures at left show some of the Heat's jerseys.

The NBA basketball is 29.5 inches (75 cm) around. It is covered with leather. The leather has small bumps called pebbles.

The pebbles on a basketball help players grip it.

TEAM STATS

Here are some of the all-time career records for the Miami Heat. These stats are complete through all of the 2018–19 NBA regular season.

GAMES

Dwyane Wade	948
Udonis Haslem	854

STEALS PER GAME

Sherman Douglas	1.70
LeBron James	1.66

ASSISTS PER GAME

Sherman Douglas	7.9
Tim Hardaway	7.8

REBOUNDS PER GAME

Hassan Whiteside	11.9
Rony Seikaly	10.4

THREE-POINT FIELD GOALS

Tim Hardaway	806
Eddie Jones	712

FREE-THROW PCT.

Ray Allen	.894
Jason Williams	.883

POINTS PER GAME

| LeBron James | 26.9 |
| Dwyane Wade | 22.7 |

29

LeBRON JAMES

GLOSSARY

dynasty *(DYE-nuh-stee)* when a team wins several championships in a row or over a period of time

expansion team *(ex-PAN-shun TEEM)* in sports, a team that is added to an existing league

franchise *(FRAN-chize)* more than just the team, the entire organization that is a member of a pro sports league

Hall of Fame *(HALL UV FAYM)* a building in Springfield, Massachusetts, that honors basketball heroes

logo *(LOW-go)* a team or company's symbol

NBA Finals *(NBA FINE-ulz)* the championship series for the NBA

playoffs *(PLAY-offs)* games played between top teams to determine who moves ahead

rivalry *(RY-vuhl-ree)* when two people or groups compete for the same thing

tank top *(TANK TOP)* a style of shirt that has straps over the shoulders and no sleeves

FIND OUT MORE

IN THE LIBRARY

Big Book of Who: Basketball (Sports Illustrated Kids Big Books). New York, NY: Sports Illustrated Kids, 2015.

Doeden, Matt. *The NBA Playoffs: In Pursuit of Basketball Glory.* Minneapolis, MN: Millbrook Press, 2019.

Goodman, Michael E. *Miami Heat (NBA Champions).* Mankato, MN: Creative Paperbacks, 2018.

ON THE WEB

Visit our website for links about the Miami Heat:
childsworld.com/links

Note to Parents, Teachers, and Librarians: We routinely verify our Web links to make sure they are safe and active sites. So encourage your readers to check them out!

INDEX

Adebayo, Bam, 20, 24
American Airlines Arena, 12, 13
Atlanta Hawks, 7
Bosh, Chris, 22, 23
Charlotte Hornets, 7, 16
court, 15
Dallas Mavericks, 16, 19
Dragic, Goran, 6
Eastern Conference, 6, 7, 11
Edwards, Kevin, 9
Houston Rockets, 9
James, LeBron, 16, 19, 22, 23
jerseys, 27
Johnson, Magic, 18
McGruder, Rodney, 10
O'Neal, Shaquille, 20, 21, 23
Orlando Magic, 7, 8, 11
Richardson, Josh, 24, 25
Southeast Division, 7, 10, 11
Wade, Dwyane, 17, 22, 23, 24
Washington Wizards, 7
Western Conference, 11
Whiteside, Hassan, 5
Winslow, Justise, 24